Say Please!

Tony Ross

Kane/Miller
BOOK PUBLISHERS

More Little Princess books

I Want My Potty
Wash Your Hands!
I Don't Want to Go to Bed!
I Want My Pacifier
I Want My Tooth

First American Edition 2006
by Kane/Miller Book Publishers, Inc.
La Jolla, CA

First published in 1995 by Andersen Press Ltd., Great Britain
Text and illustrations copyright © 1995 by Tony Ross

All rights reserved. For information contact:
Kane/Miller Book Publishers, Inc.
P.O. Box 8515
La Jolla, CA 92038
www.kanemiller.com

Library of Congress Control Number: 2006921211

Printed and bound in China by Regent Publishing Services, Ltd.

1 2 3 4 5 6 7 8 9 10

ISBN-10: 1-933605-16-2
ISBN-13: 978-1-933605-16-6

"I WANT MY DINNER!"

"Say PLEASE," said the Queen.

"I want my dinner…PLEASE."

"Mmmmm, lovely."

"I want my potty."

"Say PLEASE," said the General.

"I want my potty, PLEASE."

"Mmmmm, lovely."

"I want my Teddy…

…PLEASE," said the Princess.

"Mmmmm."

"We want to go for a walk...PLEASE."

"Mmmmm."

"Mmmmm…that looks good."

"HEY!" said the Beastie.

"That's MY dinner."

"I want my dinner!"

"Say PLEASE," said the Princess.

"I want my dinner, PLEASE."

"Mmmmm."